Party Time

Written by Catherine Baker
Illustrated by Ángeles Peinador

Collins

2

4

6

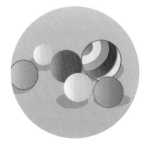  

8

10

12

Who helped get the party ready?
What did they do?

After reading

> **Letters and Sounds:** Phase 1
>
> **Word count:** 0
>
> **Curriculum links:** EYFS: Understanding the World: People and Communities
>
> **Early learning goals:** Listening and attention: children listen attentively in a range of situations; Understanding: children answer 'how' and 'why' questions about their experiences and in response to stories or events

Developing fluency

- Encourage your child to hold the book and turn the pages.
- Spend time looking at the pictures and discussing them, drawing on any relevant experience or knowledge your child has. Encourage them to talk about what they can see in each picture, giving as much detail as they can.

Phonic practice

- Look for and discuss the items in the small circles at the bottom of the pages (what noise do they make, if any?). Try to copy some of the noises using voice sounds and body percussion.
- Talk about the soft and loud noises they might hear if they were in each scene. (e.g. *blowing up a balloon, the scissors snipping the paper, the banging of a drum*)
- Look for opportunities to explore alliteration, by focusing on things in the pictures that begin with 'p' on pages 2–3, 'd' on pages 4–5, 'm' on pages 6–7, 'c' on pages 8–9, 'b' on pages 10–11 and 's' on pages 12–13.

Extending vocabulary

- Talk further about the pictures in circles at the bottom of the pages. Ask your child to tell you what they see. Can they spot the objects in the main picture?
- Discuss words for all of the things children can see in the pictures. Ask them to point out anything they don't recognise. Tell them the word for it and explain what it is.